THE TALE OF
EARTHA THE SEA TURTLE

Written by: Dan Bodenstein
Illustrated by: Brian C. Krümm

Totem Tales Publishing™
PO Box 741511
Boynton Beach, Florida 33474-1511

web: www.totemtales.com
email: books@totemtales.com

Phone: (561) 537-2522

First published by Totem Tales Publishing 11/11/2009

ISBN: 978-0-9843228-0-0

Printed in the United States of America

For information on sales and distribution, please contact:

Totem Tales Publishing™
(561) 537-2522
books@totemtales.com

In memory of Ken DuCheney.
Without whom I never would have
met the real sea turtle named Eartha.

This book is written with the approval of the
Loggerhead Marinelife Center of Juno Beach, Florida.
For more information on sea turtles
visit www.marinelife.org

The ocean is full of amazing creatures that spend their whole lives underwater. This is the story of one of those special creatures. My name is Moonfeather, and this is the tale of Eartha the Sea Turtle.

Eartha was a young sea turtle who loved to swim in the ocean. Eartha was curious about the ocean and all the wonderful things it held. She would often swim with other sea turtles or even swim and play with other fish.

While swimming through the ocean,
Eartha swam into something that she had never
seen before. It was some kind of shiny string.
First it got caught on her flipper,

and then it got caught on her shell.
Eartha tried and tried to get the string off,
but she just kept getting more and more tangled!
What is this? wondered Eartha.

More and more the string got tangled around her flippers, and her shell, making it harder for her to swim. She did her best to swim, but her flippers were hard to move with all the string on them.

Eartha swam to a nearby crab.
"Mr Crab, can you help me get this string off?"
The crab tried to cut the string, but it wouldn't cut.
"Sorry, Eartha; my claws aren't sharp enough."

She then asked her friend the squid for help.
The squid tried with all his might to pull the string
apart with his tentacles. "Sorry," said the squid.

She then asked a lobster, a passing eel,
and even her friend the clam, but none of them
was strong enough to break the string.

Sad and alone, Eartha floated to the surface
of the ocean. She didn't know what to do.
She couldn't cut the string, and none of her
sea friends were strong enough to help her.
What would she do?

Night time came, and Eartha was scared.
The moon was shining above. Eartha had always
liked the moon. She looked up at the moon and asked
it to help her. Then, Eartha began to cry.

The moon looked different to Eartha that night. As she stared at the moon, it got bigger and bigger. Suddenly, the water all around her lit up.

It was a boat! On the boat, a man was shining a
bright light on Eartha. Eartha didn't know what to do.
She couldn't swim away, because she was all tangled.
She flapped her flippers as best she could to try
to scare the boat away.

The boat didn't leave.
Instead, the man on the boat threw a net around Eartha
and gently lifted her onto the boat.

She had never been on a boat before. It seemed very dry compared to the ocean. There were people moving around her, and Eartha was scared. Then she heard a woman say, "Don't worry, turtle; we'll take care of you." The woman smiled at Eartha and that made her feel better.

Eartha still didn't know where the boat was taking her. Would she ever get to swim in the ocean again? Would she ever see her friends again? She looked at the string still wrapped around her and began to cry.

Eartha looked up at the night sky, closed her eyes, and fell asleep. That night she dreamed of playing under the sea with her friends. It was a wonderful dream.

Eartha woke up the next morning and looked at her flipper. The string was all gone and she was back in the water! She flapped her flipper all around and swam round and round in happiness.

She rose to the surface of the water and knew she
wasn't in the ocean. She was in a
water tank. She popped her head over
the edge of the tank and saw there was
another sea turtle in the next tank.

"Hi." she said, "My name is Eartha."
The other sea turtle was much older than Eartha.
He lifted his head up above his tank and said,
"My name is Roger. They call me Jolly Roger."

"Where am I?" asked Eartha.
"This is a hospital for sea turtles," explained Roger.
"These people are helping you get better.
Once you are better, they will send you back to the sea."

Eartha smiled and looked at her flipper.
She knew she was better and all the string was
gone. That meant she was going
back home, to the sea.

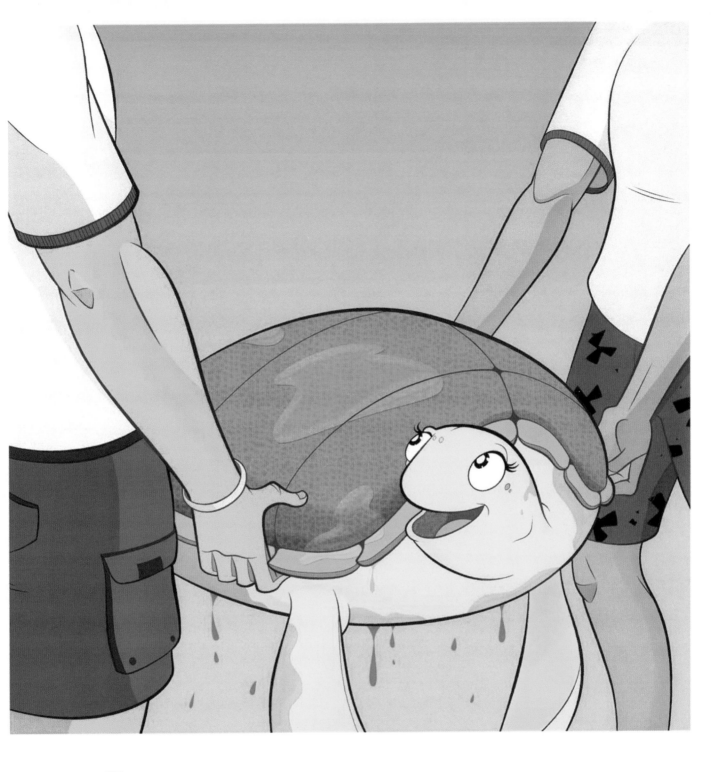

She was right! Two men approached her tank.
They reached down into the water and lifted Eartha
out of the tank and onto a long piece of wood.

They carried her down to the beach.
"Be careful," said Eartha. "Don't drop me.
I'm going home!" Eartha wasn't the only one who
knew she was going home. The beach was full of people,
and they were waiting to watch Eartha return to the sea.

The two men placed Eartha on the sand. She stretched out with her flippers and pulled herself down to the water's edge. Eartha thought about what would have happened to her if those people hadn't helped her. She realized she was lucky that there were special people in the world that cared.

Eartha looked back at all the people on the beach and said, "Thank you."

Eartha crawled down the beach to where
the sand met the water. The waves splashed her
many times, tickling her face.
This made Eartha smile and giggle.

As soon as she got into the water, she
went all the way to the bottom, zooming
along the ocean floor. Eartha was going home.

Eartha was happy. She swam as
fast as she could. She did twists and loops.
It reminded her why she loved the ocean.

She stopped to show her friends the crab, the clam, the squid, and the eel that she was all better. She explained that she had gotten twisted up in garbage from the land people. "Do all land people do that?" asked Mr. Crab. "No," said Eartha. "There are nice people and they are the ones that helped me." She explained how special those people were to her.

Eartha had learned that the sea is full of both wonders and dangers. She realized that there are good people that care about the sea and help protect all the creatures that live there.

I'm sure if you met Eartha today she would ask you,

"Are you one of those good people?"

PARENTS' PAGE

This story is based on the true story of a rescued sea turtle named Eartha. Many rescue centers have education programs designed specifically for children. Through education, we can help protect these endangered and threatened species.

Teaching our children the need to live in harmony with nature may be the most valuable lesson they can learn. Both the children and nature benefit from this shared knowledge.

To learn more about what you can do and where your child can adopt a sea turtle, visit www.EarthaTheSeaTurtle.com. There you will find resources where your childs personal adventure can begin.

"We do not inherit the land from our ancestors; we borrow it from our children."

Native American proverb

Made in the USA
Lexington, KY
19 July 2011